SUDARSHINI'S UNCAGED BIRD

GREAT MINDS

First Edition

Cover & Other Illustrations: Hanitha Devi
ISBN: 978-93-343-4821-7
Published by Great Minds

Printed In India

Dedicated to every woman, who carried strength quietly
and never failed to rise again after each fall.

CONTENTS

PROLOGUE: FROM THE AUTHOR'S HEART

In a world that often celebrates the image of a liberated woman, one who walks freely, pursues a career of her choice, lives independently, and dares to dream without fear. Do you think things changed? No, there still exist places where such freedom remains a distant hope. In certain countries, and even within the closed walls of many families, women are still expected to conform, to stay silent, to shrink themselves to fit into molds crafted by age-old traditions and expectations.

This story unfolds in the heart of India, centred on a woman who never fit the mold, and never had the luxury of freedom, not even in thought. A secluded soul weighed down by invisible chains of pain, blame, fear, and generations of conditioning. Her voice has been silenced by those around her, her dreams dismissed as foolish, and her existence confined within the rigid walls of what society says a woman should be.

But this is not merely a tale of suffering, it is a journey of strength. A journey of a woman who, despite being caged by circumstances beyond her control, learns to breathe through the bars. The story delves deep into her inner world, revealing the untold battles she fights each day, facing harsh judgments, carrying the weight of undeserved blame, suppressing her true feelings, and navigating through emotional darkness with no guide but her own willpower.

Through every obstacle, she doesn't break, she bends, adapts, survives. Her strength lies not in loud rebellion, but in quiet endurance and steady resolve. As life grows tougher, and the world around her becomes more demanding, she begins to uncover something powerful within herself, a fire that refuses to die out. A voice that, though once buried beneath years of silence, begins to rise.

This story is a tribute to every woman who has been caged, by tradition, by society, by fear, or by her own self-doubt, and yet found a way to dream. It is about the courage it takes to face the darkness, the grit it takes to keep moving, and the transformation that begins the moment she decides she will no longer live small.

This is her story—raw, real, painful, and powerful. A journey of becoming. A testament to what it truly means to rise when the world insists you stay small. It tells the story of a little girl who silenced her dreams, who yearned for love and the warmth of someone's presence. A woman who bears the weight of undeserved blame, and is constantly asked to shrink herself to fit the demands of her family and circumstances

CHAPTER 1
AT HER EARLY AGE

It was a rainy day; the entire city was engulfed in storm clouds and on the brink of heavy downpours, as conditions worsened with each passing moment, the streets became deserted. The meteorology centre had announced the increasing intensity of the cyclone. As a precaution, people living near the sea were advised to move to a safe zone, as a giant wave was expected to rise and could cause severe damage to homes along the coastline.

The wind gusted
And the giant waves raised.
It seemed as touching the sky
And produced fear in the souls.
A deep silence prevailed outside for a while,
But an intense fear prevailed inside for a long while.
All were sealed inside by storms
And united by the disaster.

A loud cry of a woman in labor pain echoed from the 7th block of the colony near the sea. Panic spread throughout the colony as everyone rushed to help. The woman was transported to the nearest town hospital and quickly taken to the delivery room. Although the umbilical cord was wrapped around the baby's neck, making the delivery complex, the doctors decided to perform an operation to save both the mother and child. After an intense struggle, the doctors successfully delivered the baby without any medical implements. However, they were surprised by the absence of a cry from the newborn and taken aback to see a smile on her face. The doctors handed the baby to her father and placed her beside her mother.

After a day, both mother and baby returned home healthy. The baby girl was named Shadvika, the second child of Varnika and Mithan. She has an elder brother, Rishidh, who is five years old. Shadvika looked like a pretty little angel with chubby cheeks and brown eyes. By her fifth month, she began crawling, much to the delight of her family.

In a few months, she transitioned from crawling to walking, and by her first birthday, she was thriving among her toys and enjoyed the love of her family every day. As time passed, she turned three and was enrolled in a convent school, marking her *first experience away from home.*

Shadvika started her school life with a pleasant smile and a sense of joy. Unlike other kids, she loved going to school and was eager to learn. Her performance in school was excellent, and she also excelled in extracurricular activities. As time went on, she turned seven, and her academic performance remained consistent. Her bond with her father deepened each day, their love was as sweet as honey and as vast as the ocean.

Shadvika made her parents proud with her remarkable achievements, scoring 90 out of 100 in science and perfect scores in her other subjects. However, her mother, Varnika, was not satisfied with her marks in science, which seemed to create a rift between them. Despite Varnika's apparent favouritism towards her first child, Shadvika chose not to dwell on it. Irrespective of the scoldings she received at home, she was often blamed for every little incident, yet she viewed these experiences as learning opportunities.

As time passed, Shadvika found solace in sculpting small figures from clay, turning this pastime into a passion. She channelled her suppressed feelings into her sculptures, each telling a story from her own life, often created in response to various triggers.

Despite being a young child, she faced many harsh circumstances. It felt as if she was disliked by everyone for no apparent reason, leaving her with a feeling of isolation even in her own home. Shadvika often felt alone, which affected her deeply. Although her family was physically present, she felt emotionally abandoned. This loneliness made her quiet wherever she went, yet even her silence was misinterpreted as arrogance by others.

Buried in the world of darkness,
The tears that welled up in silence

And dried in the pillows every night.
None of the soul gave hands.
She was pushed into the pit
That's darker and creepy.
A heart that broken into pieces,
Fallen in the pit and lost in the sea
Which cannot be fetched forever!

At a very young age, she began to wonder about the meaning of life. Her creativity blossomed day by day, and her production of small sculptures increased. However, her mother often scolded her for spending too much time on her art, which negatively impacted her academic performance. She struggled with memories from her past that weighed heavily on her, affecting both her studies and her passion for sculpting. The judgments of others whenever she opened up, deeply troubled her, even though she tried her best to push those thoughts away. Despite the challenges, she held onto hope and managed to gather herself each day, determined to pursue her dream.

Her primary desire is to become a skilled sculptor, yet her family didn't support her aspirations, believing that sculpting had no future. Nevertheless, she remained confident in her abilities and continued to sculpt, working even harder despite her mother's protests.

As the years went by, she turned 13 and began prioritizing her studies. She focused on her academics while still finding time to sculpt. Some friends had left her school, but she formed new bonds with Revika and Mritha. With the support of her friends and father, her artistic endeavours gained more recognition, and her mother started to come around as well. She was allowed to pursue her sculpting skills while also dedicating time to her studies.

Despite finding science challenging, she dedicated herself to preparing for her ninth-grade final exams. Her hard work paid off, and she was promoted to the tenth grade, gradually earning more trust from her mother.

CHAPTER 2
TEENAGE LIFE

She stepped into her teenage years and started a small sculpture business, where she began earning money. She never took a penny for herself; instead, she gave all her earnings to her parents. Her business provided a comfortable and prosperous life for her family, and she continued sculpting, even learning to work with very challenging materials. Alongside this, she focused on her studies to achieve good marks in her exams. However, she struggled to score well in science. She found the subject difficult, and her efforts didn't seem to work.

Her parents decided to hire a tutor for her to help improve her grades, but she wasn't interested in that. Determined to succeed, she embraced a new attitude and worked hard both day and night to reach the top. Her efforts paid off; she scored centum in three subjects out of five, making her parents proud, earning recognition at school. She was placed in the Arts group for higher secondary. However, this year would be even more challenging for Shadvika.

She pepped herself to overcome the new goal,
And spurred herself to achieve her target.
Now, her merely vision is the education
And to hit her target without shiver.

She started to make the most of every second, setting daily targets for herself. As June arrived, her first year of higher secondary schooling began, and the teachers raced through the syllabus like Usain Bolt. The students hurried to keep up, and soon the announcement was made: the first unit exam would take place at the end of the month. Everyone was encouraged to perform well. Shadvika motivated herself to tackle this challenge head-on. She set even tougher goals and worked diligently day and night.

As it was her first exam, she felt quite tense and anxious about making a good impression. However, she gathered her composure and successfully completed her exams. The results came out soon after, and she excelled, achieving the top position in her class.

Her classmates were astonished, and her friends felt envious, especially since she was the one who had previously received the lowest scores among the three of them. For them, seeing her score well this year seemed like a distant goal. Nevertheless, she continued to treat them as she always had. Her academic journey was filled with ups and downs, accompanied by failures and disappointments. Each setback made her more resilient.

Over time, she began to see the true nature of her friends and the insincerity in their feelings towards her. Although their hurtful emotions were difficult for her to bear, she still found motivation in their cruelty. However, she eventually detached herself from them, realizing that they were no longer friends but merely classmates.

Sometimes, some shelters you,
That is not eternal.
Some may stand by you,
But not so truly, just to get their works done.
Sometimes, you may be praised.
But who knows, it might be a pseudo one.
We remain positive every time,
But people around us often plant negative thoughts in our minds.
The one who overcome by breaking those negativity
Will be the one who wins in this world.

She again scored the best in both the grades of higher secondary and successfully completed her schooling. She faced a significant decision: choosing her undergraduate program, which would be one of the most important moves of her life and define her future. Despite her parents' wishes for her to get married, she chose to study for a Bachelor of Fine Arts (B.F.A.) in Sculpture. She stood firm against their decision, even if it meant risking a year of her education. For that year, she felt like a guest in her own home as she fought for her independence. During this time, she learned Italian, created nearly ten sculptures every day, sold them daily, and saved ₹3,50,000. She then travelled to Florence, Italy, to pursue her Bachelor of Fine Arts (B.F.A.) in Sculpture.

Her dream had come true, and all her hard work paid off with happiness. She gained admission to one of the top public universities in Italy with scholarship and began her first year of undergraduate studies with great enthusiasm. She found a house with budget-friendly rent and managed her expenses by staying there, using the money she had earned. However, lingering in her mind were feelings of guilt for leaving her parents alone. The culture in Italy was entirely different, which posed challenges for her and caused her to lose focus on her sculpting.

One day, while returning from the university, Shadvika was hit by a cycle, causing her to fall into the street. The cyclist stopped, helped her up, and they discovered that she had some scratches on her legs. The cyclist took her to a nearby clinic, where her wounds were dressed. Through their conversation, they got to know each other better.

This is how she met Shritha, another Indian girl living in Italy, who was also in her first year of B.F.A. Sculpture at a different university in Florence. A friendship blossomed between them, becoming very close. Unlike Shadvika, Shritha had also fought with her parents and left home, but she viewed sculpting purely as a form of entertainment and fun. Their bond was like a tightly knotted string, connecting the passionate one and the one who saw it as a pastime. Shadvika eventually moved in with Shritha and continued to attend her university from there. Even though it was farther from her previous home, she managed to make it work.

One weekend, they planned to visit Venice, known as "The Floating City" in Italy, where boats are the primary mode of transportation. While traveling by boat to the Gallerie dell'Accademia, Shadvika heard the most melodious song sung by a man with a peculiar voice, which captivated her. She longed to find out who he was, but unfortunately, she couldn't identify him just by the song.

During their time in Venice, they explored famous landmarks and sampled local delicacies such as Sarde in saor, Risi e bisi, and Bigoli in salsa. They wrapped up their visit around 9 p.m. and took a train to Florence, arriving at midnight.

Chapter 2: Teenage Life

Chapter 2: Teenage Life

Despite feeling tired, Shadvika attended her classes the very next day, while Shritha chose to stay home and take a break due to fatigue from her trip to Venice. When Shadvika returned home from university, she found that Shritha was out and didn't come back until the following morning. She didn't question her at first, but soon noticed that this pattern continued; Shritha would leave in the afternoon and only return the next morning.

One day, Shadvika caught Shritha in the act. It turned out that she had been going out with two Italian men in the afternoons, returning only at sunrise. Shritha's behaviour and her flirtationship with these men prompted Shadvika to distance herself from her. She advised Shritha to end her questionable activities and make better choices, but Shritha ignored her words. As a result, Shadvika grew increasingly frustrated and spent most of her time at university.

One morning, around 9 a.m., the doorbell rang while Shritha was in the shower. Shadvika went to answer the door and found one of the Italian men with whom Shritha was involved. She welcomed him inside and went to inform Shritha. Shortly after, she returned with a cup of coffee for him. Suddenly, he began to flirt with Shadvika, asked in a flirtatious manner,

"Andiamo ad un appuntamento stasera? E quanto dovrei pagare per te?" (Shall we go on a date tonight? And how much should I pay for you?)

Shadvika was furious and shouted, "Sei un bastardo!" (you bastard!), before storming into her room and slamming the door.

That incident shattered the bond between Shadvika and Shritha. Afterwards, Shadvika decided to leave Shritha's home and move back to the house she stayed. The event affected her deeply and troubled her greatly. Although Shritha apologized for what had happened, Shadvika was no longer interested in forgiving her.

Feeling lonely and missing her family, Shadvika spent her days focusing on her sculpting work and having Skype calls with her parents. Despite her sense of isolation, she found the strength to energize herself and pursue her passion.

CHAPTER 3
KNOWN BUT UNKNOWN

When she was set to visit Ponte Vecchino and explore the shops along the bridge, she suddenly heard the same enchanting voice that had mesmerized her in Venice, accompanied by the same song. Eagerly, she rushed towards the source of the melodious sound, but halfway there, the music came to an abrupt stop. She paused, a wave of disappointment washing over her.

Chapter 3: Known But Unknown

On the next sunrise, she washed her hair, polished her nails, and enhanced the beauty of her eyes by applying all kinds of eye cosmetics like eyeliner, mascara, soft beige shades of eyeshadows, and to her lips applied the sepia brown lipstick to attend her college music event, **The Concert of Brihant**, An Indian but a famous musician in Italy.

It is her desire to attend his concert from the day when she came to Italy and heard about him for the first time from her classmates. Even though a lot of his tracks were available on Spotify, she was determined to only listen to his songs at his live concert, and should not listen to any of his songs until then. She knew a list of his songs, but never heard those and never knew how his voice would be. She was euphoric about attending the concert that going to happen at her university, which is completely free of cost. She rushed into the concert hall and her feet were off from the ground.

On the deep silence
Heard the voice of him
The one that is familiar
The one that mesmerized her already.
Her eyes ran towards the stage
On the stage, between the dazzling lights
Saw a man with a lion walk.

A man passion filled,
With perfectly separated black hair
With stubble beard and peculiar voice.
Her eyes gaped
At the moment when he is on her sight,
Her soul melted to his song
And she is out of the world.

The concert ended, and she was just dumbstruck by his performance as well as by the truth that his voice was the one that attracted her in Venice. The management took Brihant to show him the best sculptures by the students. In those, one of the works mesmerized him, the sculpture that portrays the pain of the artists to shine. He wondered at the sculpture and asked, “Who is the sculptor of this work?”
“It was sculptured by one of the best students of our university and her name is Shadvika” replied one of the management people.

His secretary was told by him to collect her contact number to get the sculpture of his choice ready. While he was set to return, she stood at the doorstep of the university among the jam-packed who were waiting to click a snap with him, but unlike everyone, she stood there to get an answer to her long-time question, not to take a snap with him. The humblest man allowed each to click a snap with him and when it was her turn

"Yeah, take a picture," he said, looking at the floor, eager to snap photos with others.

"No, sir, I don't want a picture with you," she replied. With astonished eyes, he looked at her face. Her beautiful eyes captivated him inexplicably, and his heartbeat felt unique, unlike anything he had experienced before. "Then?" he asked tenderly, with love-filled eyes.

"I want to ask you something," she replied.

"Sure," he said.

"In every interview, you have been asked, 'Why don't you get close to the people around you?' Your only answer has always been that anyone who becomes close to you will either have a fight and leave permanently or, after a disagreement, the bond diminishes and will never feel the same again. If I'm right in thinking that's the reason you avoid getting close to anyone, have you ever considered that there might be someone who could stay with you forever? Or have you ever noticed that even after a fight, there's a person who remains in your life as before, with no decrease in bonding or feeling? If so, could you tell me who that person is?" she asked.

He was left dumbstruck by her question, only able to stare at her with astonishment and no answers to give. He left the place in a daze, bewildered and without a response. She wondered if she had asked something inappropriate.

Weeks passed, and one day, when she returned from university, her phone rang, seems to be an unknown number. She answered, “Hello?” “Is this Shadvika?” a voice on the other end asked.
“Yes,” she replied.
“I’m the secretary of a musician. We need a unique musical instrument sculpture for our studio,” the secretary explained. Shadvika was shocked and accepted the project, but when the call ended, she realized she had forgotten to ask for the musician’s name. She didn’t dwell on the details and quickly began her work.

For days and nights, without break, she worked hard to create the best piece possible. After nearly three weeks of effort, she was almost finished with her sculpture in the fourth week. The highlight of this story is that she was sculpting for her favourite musician, Brihant, without knowing whose studio she was creating for. Meanwhile, he was unaware that the sculptor and the girl who had questioned him were the same person, Shadvika.

Chapter 3: Known But Unknown

Once the sculpture was delivered to Brihant studio, he was captivated by it the moment he saw it. The secretary invited Shadvika to lunch at Brihant's home, but unfortunately, she had important commitments at her university. She was invited to come for lunch whenever she became free, and Brihant, enchanted by her sculpture, wanted to meet her. Yet again, she forgot to ask for the musician's name.

When she finally became free and was ready to go for lunch at his home, he had become busy with work, and their meeting was cancelled once more. Each time they attempted to meet, it fell through for various reasons, and again she missed to ask for his name.

He remained unaware of who she was; he knew her as the sculptor but did not realize that she was the same girl who had questioned him at his last concert. She remained unknown to him, while she was known to him. Their every attempt to meet was cancelled, and they both accepted their fate, letting things be as they were. She never asked for his name, and whenever they spoke on the phone, she could not recognize his voice.

Will he discover that the girl who questioned him and the sculptor are the same person? And will she find out that she created a sculpture for her favourite musician? What will their fate be?

CHAPTER 4
MUSICULPTURE

On one side, he was filled with love for the girl who had questioned him, and on the other, she was captivated by the sound of his voice. Both souls were in love with each other, connected without their awareness. Although their planned meetings had been cancelled, fate arranged a meeting they could not avoid.

As she was returning from college and he was heading to the studio, the rain blurred the view through his car window. Amid the mist, he saw her glowing like a star. He stopped the car and walked towards her, love shining in his eyes. When she met his gaze, he felt as though he could see his whole world reflected in hers. She was filled with excitement at the sight of him, while he was overwhelmed by his feelings. Unbeknownst to him, she was the sculptor of the piece he has in his studio.

They gazed at each other in silence for a moment, communicating with their eyes. "Can we have coffee together?" he asked. "Yes," she replied. They went to the nearest café and ordered hot coffee to warm themselves in the cold weather. Sitting opposite each other, he admired her beauty, lost in love, unaware that she noticed. When the hot coffee arrived, he regretted that it came too soon, interrupting his gaze.

After finishing their drinks, they prepared to leave the café and walked together until they reached her house. Once there, she discovered that he didn't know her name.
"May I know your name?" he asked.
"Shadvika, sir," she replied.

He was dumbstruck and left without saying another word, leaving her perplexed by his strange behaviour. He was surprised to learn that she was the sculptor of the beautiful piece in his studio. His love for her grew, and he was once again mesmerized by her talent. In his enthusiasm, he thought she must have known she sculpted it for him.

The next day, they met again at the same spot unexpectedly. They went to Parco Villa Vogel and sat on a bench under the shade of the trees.
"Why did you leave without saying anything? Did my name scare you?" she asked.
"No!" he replied with a smile.
"Did you order a sculpture for your studio?" she inquired.

Her question made him realize that she was unaware of the musician for whom she had sculpted. Since his secretary had handled the order; he decided to keep it a surprise for her. "No," he replied.

They exchanged phone numbers, and their bond began to grow closer. They spent the entire evening at Parco Villa Vogel, talking and enjoying each other's company before finishing their dinner at a nearby restaurant. As they got into the car to head home, she was exhausted and leaned her head against the car window, falling asleep.

After a few minutes, he noticed her and gently moved her head to rest on his shoulder while holding her hand. He admired her closed eyes, glowing lips, and pretty cheeks. Just as he leaned in to kiss her hand, she woke up, realizing they had arrived at her house. With a blush on her face, she hurriedly got out of the car and walked coyly towards her front door. Once inside, she tossed her bag aside and rushed to the mirror, noting how cute she looked. heart beat touched the sky. She felt like

A butterfly bitten her neck,
Chewed her sugar lips,
Kissed her cheeks,
Pinched her hip
And tried to make her fall for its scent.

Chapter 4: Musiculpture

She freshened up and got ready for bed. It was 12 a.m., then 1 a.m., 3 a.m., and finally 6 a.m., she had spent the entire night without any sleep. She rolled around in her bed but could not fall asleep. The next day, she spent the whole day yawning with sleepy eyes.

When she returned from college, she decided it would be best not to meet him that day, as she was certain he would be on her way home. She wrapped her face in a shawl, leaving only her eyes exposed, and walked hesitantly. However, he did not cross her path that day.

Once she reached home, she reflected on why she felt the need to hide her face and why she was afraid of him. Looking at herself in the mirror, she spoke to herself, "One incident doesn't define a person. It could have happened accidentally. He likely didn't mean anything by it; I must have misunderstood him." She resolved to act normally the next time they met.

But they didn't see each other for more than a couple of days. She was busy with her exams, and he had his own commitments. Days turned into weeks, and neither of them had a conversation, whether in person, by chat, or through calls. A week passed, and then two months went by, still, they had not met or communicated. She began to think about it a lot.

Some days, she thought that he feels embarrassing to talk to her,
Some days she thought that he behaved in such a way to mean something,
Some days with the thought of he is innocent.
And, some days with the thought of he is interested in her.
her muse prolonged with no rest

Not even for a second, a minute and an hour.

A lot of questions raced through her mind, and even though she decided to stop thinking about his recent behaviour, she found it impossible to let go. Every time she watched a movie, it reminded her of that incident. Through her observations, she partially understood that he might have an interest in her, but she wasn't entirely sure.

Over the course of four months, she felt as if she was trapped in a maze. She had just completed her first year of graduation, and during those months, they had a few conversations, but they were nothing like the ones they'd had before the incident. She sensed fear in his voice, and he often avoided their conversations by pretending to be overwhelmed with work. This behaviour sometimes made her feel neglected. Yet, part of her believed he was hiding his feelings for her.

She still couldn't explain his sudden change in behaviour. It bothered her and made her feel avoided. After those four months, they lost touch. She began to miss him and worry about him for no apparent reason. She couldn't get through a single minute without thinking of him. These thoughts disrupted her, and she realized, without fully recognizing it, that she had fallen for him. As a result, she decided to distance herself from him, as her concentration on sculpting was suffering. The second year of her graduation began, fuelled by her passion for sculpting and her determination to improve her skills. Her love for the art transformed her sculptures, infusing them with emotion. The entire university marvelled at her work, and they fell in love with her sculpture, which beautifully captured the essence of motherly love and the bond between a mother and child.

Her sculpture was celebrated as the most captivating piece at the university and was selected for display at the prestigious Venice Biennale, Italy's most renowned art exhibition held every two years, often attended by the President of Italy and other distinguished figures. The most admired artworks at this event are sometimes acquired by collectors and cultural institutions.

Excited yet nervous, she felt a mix of jubilation and apprehension. Her sculpture became highly regarded at the exhibition, attracting everyone's attention. It was the moment of the President's arrival; his car parked right in front of the entrance to the exhibition hall. He stepped out, flanked by about ten bodyguards. No one could approach him or speak to him. Shadvika was stunned when she saw the President. He glanced at the works on display, and as he drew closer to her sculpture, her anxiety intensified. Finally, when the President stood before her sculpture, he stared at it in amazement and said, "I've never seen anything like this before. I feel a bond with this piece." Then he added warmly, "I want to purchase this sculpture for €1,000." He also requested her autograph. Shadvika was taken aback; it felt like a dream she couldn't believe was real. Trembling, she held the pen and made her first autograph for the President. She had never imagined she would receive recognition from someone so prominent. In that moment, she felt like she was sitting on a throne, empowered and validated. Unbeknownst to her, this would be the first step towards becoming an inspiration for many in the future.

Her sculpture quickly became popular, going viral on every social media platform. The President of Italy even tweeted about her work with credits, accompanied by a photograph. This news reached every corner of India and beyond. News channels ran headlines like "The Sculpture of the Youngest Indian Sculptor Captivates the President of Italy," shining a spotlight on both the sculpture and the artist.

Her parents beamed with pride, and her work inspired aspiring artists across the country to pursue sculpting. Yet, amid her joy, she experienced a pang of longing, as she hadn't received any congratulatory message from Brihant. She waited for over a week, anxiously checking her notifications every time her phone buzzed, hoping it would be a message from him. It had been a month, yet she had received neither a message nor a call from him...

CHAPTER 5
A NEW STAR IN THE SKY

A new star was born in Shadvika, who has now risen as the queen of her own life. Although she has been honoured and widely recognized, this fame has not significantly influenced her mindset, and she has chosen not to place much importance on popularity. While people regard her as a famous person, she continues to live simply and has refused to seek wealth.

Her respect for everyone has remained unchanged, and the events that have unfolded in her life have not altered her character. On October 16, as it drizzled outside, Shadvika was busy sculpting a tree that one of her customers had ordered to be placed in their garden. She was determined to complete the order by the end of the day. Suddenly, the doorbell rang. "Coming!" Shadvika called out. She went to the door and received a package from the postman, feeling a bit curious about its contents.

When she unwrapped it, she found a letter from one of her fans, but there was no name attached. Excitement filled her as she realized it was her first letter from a fan. Her eyes sparkled with enthusiasm as her hands eagerly opened the letter in a joyful rush.

Dear Sculptor,

I hope you are doing well. I am incredibly excited about all your works and am mesmerized by your kind heart. You have a unique place in my heart. You are the one who ignited my love through your art. Your smile makes me smile every day, and your happiness brings me joy each day. I feel entrapped by your sculptures, as if I have become a sculpture myself, shaped by the good-hearted sculptor. You have taken me to a world of imagination and taught me the value of the bond between a mother and child. It is you, the great sculptor, who has changed my life and illuminated my path. I will always be devoted to your stunning sculptures, and my eyes will long for you until my last breath.

From,
The person who loves you endlessly

The words expressed by her fan inspired her to improve and shine like the only star in the sky. She was eager to discover the identity of the person who sent the letter and felt euphoric at the thought of meeting that person. As the day passed, the very next morning, the doorbell rang. When she opened the door, she found a bouquet on the doorstep with a note, "From the person who loves you endlessly." It was the same person who had sent her the letter the previous day. She received a new gift every Sunday, and her curiosity to meet the person grew, even though she didn't know anything about the person, not the gender or age.

Her undergraduate studies came to an end, and she turned 21. It was time for her to return to India, but she felt fearful about going back because she knew her family would want to arrange her marriage, something she dreaded. Additionally, she was burdened with an abundance of unexpressed love for Brihant. Two years of no communication with him had made her realize her deep love for him. She feared that they might never be together and questioned whether she could live the rest of her life without him. Though she wanted to meet him, her fear prevented her from gathering the strength to see and talk to him.

She informed her family about her upcoming return home and breathed in the air of India after three years. Her family celebrated her homecoming with joy, and the whole house was filled with lights and festive cheer. She felt joyful about their warm welcome. A few hours later, as she sat down for lunch after everyone else, her mother, Varnika, sat beside her and asked, "Shadvika, I don't know how you are going to take this, but first let me ask you a question. Do you love someone?" Shadvika glanced at her mother nervously, and before she could respond, her mom continued, "I know you very well, my child. You wouldn't do that, am I right?" With a slight smile, Shadvika replied, "Yes, you're right."

Her mother's words left her feeling blue, as she sensed that they were planning to arrange her marriage. She retreated to her room and wept over her unexpressed feelings for Brihant and her fear of not being able to confess her love to him.

On that night standing in the terrace,
Raising her head towards the sky
With so much of pain in her heart.
She saw the star in the sky
To her eyes twinkled only two
That just glimmers like him and her,
But she found it is separated by the miles
And hoping to brought together by the times.

It was around 8:00 a.m. when the smell of coffee from the kitchen woke her up from her sleep. She got out of bed and headed directly to the kitchen. There, she found her mother preparing coffee. She quickly brushed her teeth, and once she finished, her mother served her a cup of hot coffee. After enjoying a nice cup of coffee, she planned to do some gardening, but just then, she heard the doorbell ring. Curious, she went downstairs to see who it was and found a courier man holding a package addressed to her. She accepted the delivery, but there was no name on the package. Unwrapping it, she discovered an Oxford blue saree adorned with chamki work, along with a letter inside.

Hello, dear. I hope you saw the saree in the package. I want you to wear this saree and get ready tonight without fail.

From,
Yours Forever

Shadvika was perplexed about who had sent her the saree and the letter. She wondered if it was the same person who had written to her before. However, the location left her confused; the letter writer is in Italy, while she is in India now. She felt surprised and eager to find out the sender's identity. As instructed, she wore the saree, applied her makeup, and got ready.

When Shadvika stepped out of her room and went downstairs, she found the living room empty. As she was about to enter the dining room, someone from behind covered her eyes with a cloth. She shouted,

"Who is this? Who are you?" The person held her hand and leaned in close, whispering, "Shhhhh!" She recognized it was a man's voice. Shadvika stopped shouting and decided to wait for him to make his move.

He slowly led her out of the house, locked the door, and ushered her into a car. As he drove to a restaurant, Shadvika tried multiple times to remove the cloth from her eyes, but he clasped her hands tightly and wouldn't let go. Once the restaurant arrived, he let her out of the car and guided her inside. The restaurant was empty except for her mom, dad, and brother. Her family was waiting for her at one of the tables.

He positioned her near the table and removed the cloth from her eyes. When she opened her eyes, the first thing she did was look at the man standing in front of her. Her eyes widened in shock as her entire world seemed to pause for a moment. The man was Brihant, and her family was filled with joy, standing alongside Brihant's family: his mother Aaravi, father Vikranth, and younger sister Bhrithi. Shadvika was still in disbelief, trying to comprehend what was happening. Varnika stepped forward and said, "This is Brihant, the groom we found for you. He will be your partner for life, and this is his family, who will be yours hereafter." Shadvika smiled but felt like she was floating with happiness inside. From her mother's conversation, she discovered that she was unaware of their previous meetings in Italy. As their families began to chat, they left Shadvika and Brihant alone outside the restaurant to talk.

Standing there in nervous anticipation, Shadvika felt a rush of fear and excitement as Brihant stepped forward, pulled out a ring box, and said, "Shadvika, I want to see your beautiful eyes every day. Please don't think I'm selfish; I wish to be the only one in your heart. I envision my future with you. Will you give me a place in your precious heart? Will you be my forever charm?" Shadvika's heart raced, and she was at a loss for words. Her suppressed emotions burst forth, and she hugged him tightly, expressing her love without needing to say anything.

Brihant felt overwhelmed with joy. They hugged for over a minute before he slipped the pave diamond ring onto her finger and gently pulled her close. "Today is my 26th birthday, and you are the best gift I could ever have. I thank God for bringing you into my life. I will love you endlessly." As she gazed at him, she realized he was the one who had sent her letters in Italy and the saree she wore.

Their moment was interrupted by a cough nearby, breaking their gaze. It was Bhrithi, who had come to speak with her future sister-in-law. She asked Brihant to step inside so she could talk with Shadvika privately. Bhrithi shared her experiences of married life, which surprised Shadvika as she thought Bhrithi was unmarried, despite their similar age.

"My marriage ended in divorce," Bhrithi began. "I got married when I was 20, last year. We were together for a year, but it wasn't what I expected. My in-laws always doubted my every action, even my husband did. They created stories about me having an affair and made a controversy out of my life. I never wanted the divorce. He was a good guy but was manipulated by his family, which led to the end of our marriage. I still remember how he loved me. Even though it was an arranged marriage, our bond felt unique. People who observed us believed we had a love marriage. I still remember his beautiful words, as well as those that shattered my heart.

I am sharing this with you because I want my brother's life to be different. I know you both love each other, but if you ever hear any rumours about him, remember to communicate openly with him instead of believing them. I hope you won't leave my brother," Bhrithi said before stepping away.

They celebrated Brihant's birthday with cake and shared a lovely dinner together. Then, Brihant drove Shadvika home. When she unlocked the door, she knew her life was about to change forever.

CHAPTER 6
HE AND SHE

Between the tall vases piled with hydrangeas on the carpet laid upon the sand, Shadvika walked in an emerald green saree with a copper border. Her blouse was intricately designed with beads and threads, and "BRISHA" was embroidered along the borders of both sleeves. The guests' eyes, focused on her, followed her until she reached the stage adorned with roses and lights. There, they tied their knot in front of their relatives, parents, and siblings. Tears of joy filled her eyes. He hugged her tightly, and his eyes conveyed a message: *no matter what, he would always be by her side.*

After completing all the rituals, Shadvika was taken to the groom's home and left there. Before departing, Varnika whispered in Shadvika's ear, "Leave all that sculpting behind. You are married now, so help your mother-in-law with household chores, cook for your family, and try to give them an heir soon." Varnika's words made Shadvika anxious, and she couldn't shake the feeling that married life might trap her once again. Brihant noticed that she seemed disturbed. On their wedding night, when she entered the room, he stopped her and asked about her gloomy demeanor. She smiled and concealed her pain behind that smile.

"Nothing, honey. I'm just tired," she replied, hugging him.

"No worries; everything will be alright if you sleep," he reassured her.

She slept beside him, and he admired his sleeping bride throughout the night. The next day, Brihant noticed that she still looked sad. Without letting her know, he decided to take her to his mother's home. He was unaware that her sadness stemmed from her mother, something she did not want to express. Shadvika entered the home normally and spent time there, while Brihant and Rishidh talked. Rishidh suspected that this marriage was either an arranged marriage or a love marriage. He had wondered about it since the day Brihant approached Shadvika's family in her absence.

"How do you know my sister? Where did you see her? Did she know you before?" Rishidh asked.

"We both have known each other for the past two years, and I fell in love with her the day I met her. However, I didn't confess my feelings. Even your sister loved me secretly. So, I decided to approach your family and later her," Brihant explained.

Rishidh smiled and said, “So, you both loved each other without expressing it... Interesting.”

Rishidh felt happy that she had created an opportunity to complicate Shadvika's life. When they left the house, Rishidh informed his parents that Shadvika and Brihant had been in love for the past two years. He claimed this entire marriage was Shadvika's plan; she had orchestrated the approach to make it look like an arranged marriage to conceal their love.

Believing him, his parents turned against Shadvika. They made her a call, and a heated argument ensued. Shadvika's family overheard the conversation. “From now on, you have no mother, father, or brother. Forget us and don't return home. You are no longer our daughter,” Varnika declared. Her words struck Shadvika deeply. She cut the call and collapsed to the ground, tears streaming down her face. Brihant and his family fell silent, feeling the weight of the situation.

Two days passed, and Shadvika neither slept nor ate. Brihant, upset by her distress, sat beside her with a plate of chapati and vegetable kurma. “My charm, don’t think you don't have anyone. I am here for you. My parents are your parents too, and my sister is a sister to you. So please, don't feel alone. Your parents maybe misunderstanding things; every misunderstanding can be resolved with time. Please eat something for me," he said gently. Her lips curved into a slight smile, and he lovingly fed her. He made her rest on his shoulder, kissed her forehead, and cared for her throughout the night.

Months went by, but Brihant noticed Shadvika had still not recovered; she remained gloomy. Although she smiled on the outside, he sensed her hidden tears. She had stopped all her sculpting work and felt idle. In hopes of reviving her spirit and helping her focus on her art, Brihant planned to take her back to Italy. Brihant's family was supportive and allowed them to follow their wishes.

Once in Italy, a surprise awaited Shadvika. Brihant's studio and their home were on the same compound. When Shadvika entered the compound, she was stunned to see a sculpture that she had created. It was for Brihant's studio! Overjoyed, she entered the house, her happiness radiating. Seeing her joyful face brought Brihant happiness as well. He opened an office for Shadvika next to Brihant's studio. She started to receive many orders, which kept her busy and helped her distance herself from her past pain.

Chapter 6: He And She

Years passed, and Shadvika and Brihant returned to India. Upon their arrival, they were surprised to find that Aaravi and Vikrant did not welcome Shadvika.

Tired from their travels, they decided not to make a big deal out of it. After resting for a few hours and freshening up, they went downstairs for lunch, only to discover that Aaravi and Vikrant had already finished eating. Aaravi came out of the kitchen, served Brihant, and then left the room. Shadvika felt downcast by Aaravi's behaviour. It had been two days since her arrival, and neither Vikrant nor Aaravi had spoken to her. She felt treated like a stranger.

Brihant noticed the tension and decided to bring Shadvika and his mother together in the living room. He made them sit opposite each other and asked Aaravi, “Mom, what’s the issue? Why aren’t you talking to Shadvika? What has she done?” Aaravi remained silent despite Brihant's repeated questions.

Finally, Aaravi shouted, “It’s been a year since you both got married, and you still don’t have a child. She is unfit for this family.” Hearing this, Vikrant came out of the room. Brihant asked him the same question, and he gave a response similar to Aaravi's.

"We did everything for your happiness, but you both didn't make us happy by giving us an heir. It seems like she married you just for money and fame, not to have a family. She has already betrayed her own parents who raised her; we are just her in-laws, so we cannot trust her. Divorce her, Brihant. She is useless and is just using you for her own needs," said Aaravi and Vikrant.

Shadvika felt shattered, and with tears in her eyes, she got up from the couch and unsteadily made her way to the upstairs room. Brihant, filled with anger, shouted, "Just stop! Nobody has the right to speak about her like that. She will be my forever. I won't

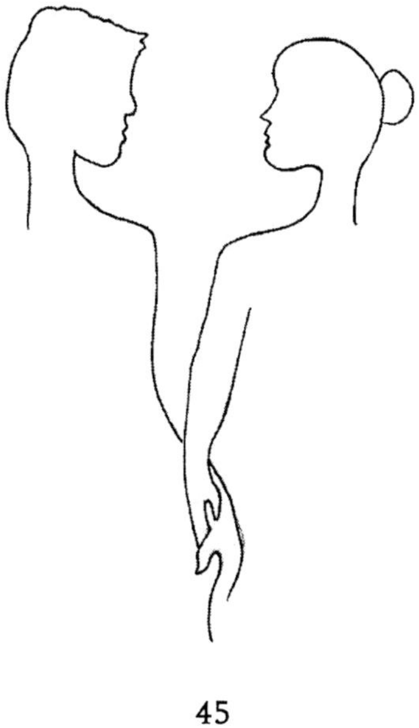

leave her at any cost, and I don't need anyone insisting that I do. Goodbye!" He stormed to his room, packed their belongings, and left the house with Shadvika. They stayed at a nearby hotel before flying away to Italy once again.

Shadvika shed tears throughout the journey, her heart feeling so heavy that no one could carry it. Brihant tried to comfort her, giving her a tight hug and a shoulder to cry on. He promised that he would never leave her side. To keep her busy, he asked each of his friends to get a new number and call her daily, placing sculpture orders so she wouldn't grow suspicious. He knew that sculpting was the only thing that could truly bring her peace. Quietly, Brihant paid his friends every order later, just to see her hands move with purpose again.

As the days passed, her worries gradually began to fade. One night, after completing her sculpting work, Shadvika returned home and went to her room to freshen up.

Standing in front of the mirror
In a spaghetti strap tank top
She wiped her face after a soak
Her Daisy hip called the thirsty lip

Of home returned him.
He cupped her hip from behind,
Kissed her neck with his dry lips
She turned towards him in faint
On his scent.
Her left hand on his chest,
His left hand on her hip.
Her right hand grabbed his hair,
His right hand clasped her back.
Both held themselves tight
He tasted her lips the whole night.

Chapter 6: He And She

They had a wonderfully dreamy night after their wedding. When she opened her eyes, she found herself sleeping on his chest. She smiled at the sleeping prince, and without disturbing him, she gently lifted his hands and slipped out of bed.

After brushing her teeth and taking a shower, she dressed and made her way to the kitchen. She boiled milk, turned off the stove, added coffee powder to two mugs, poured in the boiled milk, and dropped in sugar cubes. The aroma of the coffee stirred Brihant from his slumber, and he came to the kitchen, hugging her from behind and whispering, "Good morning, my charm," in a sleepy voice. Her lips spread into a smile as she turned to him, kissed his forehead, and said, "Sweet morning, Amore. Your coffee is ready."

Just then, her phone rang, and she dashed to pick up the call. It was from one of her favourite actresses in Italy, wanting her to create ten decorative sculptures for her new home, for which she would be paid €204365. She was over the moon! As soon as she ended the call, she rushed back to Brihant, hugged him tightly, and expressed her excitement. From that night on, she immersed herself in her work, sculpting day and night without much rest. Occasionally, she would fall asleep at her office, and Brihant would carry her to their bedroom, tuck her hair behind her ear, cover her with the blankets, turn off the lights, and then return to bed himself.

Their life continued smoothly with busy schedules. Shadvika successfully completed the ten decorative sculptures within two months and delivered them to the actress who had placed the order. However, just as everything seemed to be going well, a storm hit Shadvika hard. One morning, as she checked her Instagram while sipping coffee, she burst into tears upon seeing her brother's wedding picture. In the photo, her family appeared happy, with not a hint of sadness for not inviting their only daughter.

Seeing Shadvika's tear-filled eyes as he came out from the bedroom, Brihant rushed to her side, asking, "What happened, my charm? Why are you in tears?" She showed him the picture, and he felt a wave of sympathy for her. He wrapped her in a warm embrace, saying, "Shadvika, I'm here for you. Don't feel down. We'll create a family that brings you happiness and pushes away all your worries." She gave him a quick kiss on the lips and smiled up at him. "Come on, let's celebrate the successful completion of your sculpture order for the actress. Let's go out for dinner tonight," he suggested. With a cheerful smile, she replied, "Yes, of course, Amore."

As evening approached, she began preparing for their dinner date. After refreshing herself, she slipped into a black slip dress. When Brihant returned home from the studio and saw his wife looking stunning, he was momentarily taken aback. He walked over to her gently, overwhelmed, and pulled her close, kissing her passionately.

"Can't you wait until after our dinner date?" she asked, playfully stopping him.

"No, I can't," he answered breathlessly, trying to kiss her again.

She pushed him away and said, "Go take a shower and get ready for our date. Let's continue this after dinner; don't spoil my look until then."

He quickly freshened up, donning a black linen shirt and white pants, and they headed to **Club del Doge** for dinner. They relished the risotto, a famous dish from the restaurant, and returned home around 10:00 p.m.

As Shadvika entered their home, she input the passcode and walked in. Brihant, who closed the door behind them, pulled her towards him and asked, "Shall we continue what we left unfinished before our date?" She stared at him in silence, a smile playing on her lips. He lifted her chin and gazed into her eyes,

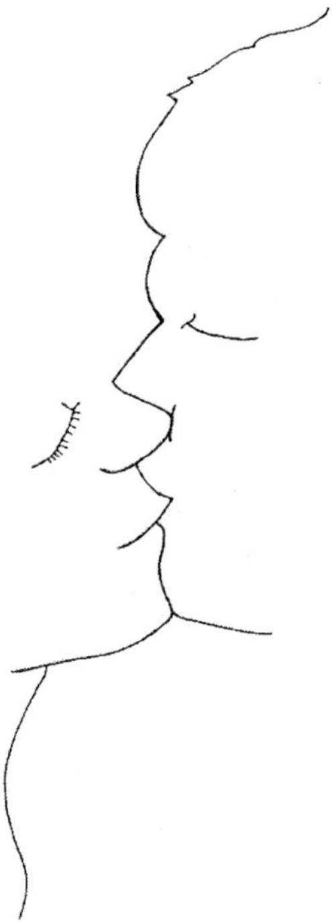

saying, "You don't need to say anything, but please don't stop me, my charm," and then he embraced her in a fiery kiss.

She unbuttoned his shirt, and he pushed her against the wall, kissing her neck fiercely. He carried her to the bedroom and laid her down on the bed. He peeled off his shirt, revealing not only his body but also the quiet vulnerability that only she ever saw. Gently, he slid the straps of her dress off her shoulders, letting the fabric fall gracefully. With a soft touch, he traced one strap down her arm, the dress slipping away like a whisper.

His lips soon followed, pressing tender kisses along her bare arm and lingering at her shoulder, then trailing to the curve of her neck and beyond, as if memorizing every inch of her with reverence. She closed her eyes, her breath catching as his lips explored her skin.

"You make me feel like I'm the only woman in the world. I wish this night could last forever... that the sun would never rise again. I just want this moment, this feeling to stretch on until my very last breath," she murmured, her voice barely above a whisper.

"As you wish, my charm. Nothing could hold me back tonight," he whispered in her ear.

Her lips curved into a gentle smile, and she drifted off to sleep in his arms, remaining there all through the night.

CHAPTER 7
A NEW BLOOM

Years passed in a blur. One calm evening, Shadvika returned home after finishing her sculpting work. Feeling a slight headache, she decided to prepare a cup of coffee. Suddenly, she felt drowsy and slowly made her way to the couch to sit down. After taking a sip of her coffee, she rushed to the sink and vomited. Concerned about what was happening, she checked her calendar and realized that her period was late this month.

Worried but hopeful, she went to a nearby pharmacy and purchased a pregnancy test kit. After taking the test at home, she was overwhelmed with happiness when she saw two lines confirming her pregnancy. Excited to share the news, she eagerly awaited Brihant's return.

When Brihant came home, he noticed that the house was dimly lit. On the living room centre table, he found a small cake with a candle on top. As he approached the cake, he read the inscription: "You're promoted to Dad." Tears of joy filled his eyes as he absorbed the news.

In that moment, the lights in the room turned on, revealing Shadvika standing beside him. He hugged her tightly, kissed her forehead, and said, "This is one of the moments of my life I will never forget. Let's cut the cake and celebrate this happiness!" They blew out the candles, cut the cake, and shared a slice together, filled with joy and anticipation for the future.

Moments of joy entered their life,
Each trimester, they celebrated with festive delight.
They furnished the room with tender care,
Preparing to welcome the tiny feet,
That would life their joy to the endless peaks.

It was her third trimester, and during the ninth month of her pregnancy, they planned to celebrate the upcoming arrival of their baby, Brihant decided to organize a baby shower at home for her. He invited his friends in Italy and sent an invite to his sister in India, hoping she could attend.

On the day of the baby shower, all of Brihant's friends arrived with their wives to bless Shadvika. When the doorbell rang, Brihant went to open it and was dumbstruck to see his sister's arrival for the baby shower. He hugged her warmly and welcomed her inside. Throughout the ceremony, Shadvika was filled with joy; seeing her sister-in-law come all the way from India made her feel on cloud nine. The baby shower ended successfully, and Brihant busily attended to his friends.

Later, Bhirithi took Shadvika to a room to help her undress and remove her ornaments. “Thank you so much for coming. I didn’t expect you to make it,” said Shadvika.

“You're my sister-in-law; how could I not come?” Bhrithi replied with a smile.

“By the way, did they tell you if the baby is a girl or a boy?” Bhrithi asked.

“They said it’s a baby boy,” Shadvika replied.

“I will be staying here until my nephew is born. Is that okay?” she asked, looking at Shadvika hopefully.

“What are you asking? You have to stay until I deliver him. You’re more important to be here. You must stay,” Shadvika ordered playfully.

“Okay, madam,” Bhrithi replied with a grin.

Days passed, and it was finally delivery day. Bhrithi waited outside the labor ward in a panic while Brihant was inside with Shadvika.

“Push, push!” the doctor shouted.

“Don’t give up! I’m here with you, my charm,” Brihant encouraged her.

Chapter 7: A New Bloom

After much effort, Shadvika successfully gave birth to a baby boy. Both she and Brihant felt a wave of joy upon hearing their baby's first cry. Nurse bathed the newborn, and when Brihant held him for the first time, he felt the tiny foot touch his chest, filling him with overwhelming happiness.

He walked out of the room holding the baby and handed him to Bhrithi. With a heart full of joy, she cradled the baby and said, "Hello, my dear nephew! Welcome to the world." Turning to Brihant, she added, "He resembles you, Brihant."

Shadvika was later moved to the regular ward with the baby. A few of Brihant's friends visited the hospital to see the baby. At this moment, Shadvika missed her family the most.

After three days, they were ready to leave the hospital and go home. Bhrithi was sent ahead to prepare for their arrival. When they entered their home, Shadvika was met with an unexpected surprise; her mother-in-law, Aaravi, was standing at the entrance to welcome her and the baby. Upon seeing her, Shadvika was overwhelmed with tears of joy.

Aaravi welcomed them home, took the baby from Shadvika's hands, and guided her to sit down.

"I'm so sorry, dear. I hurt you with my words," Aaravi said.

"That's okay, Mom," Shadvika replied, trying to reassure her.

"I have been too harsh with you, yet you still call me 'Mom,'" Aaravi said with a smile, pulling Shadvika into a warm hug.

Their life bloomed fresh,
All the pain vanished,
All the misunderstanding didn't stand anymore,
All the bitters vanished,
Instead, life started to offer them sweets.
Smile prolonged in the lips of them,
Painstream is replaced with gleestream.
Cry of the baby echoed everywhere,
Their delight added lights to the house,
Made the house the brightest of the street.

Three months flew by, and they found themselves in India. They arranged a baby naming ceremony, inviting Brihant's family, his friends, and Shadvika's friends. Even in that happy moment, her eyes remained fixed on the WhatsApp message she had sent to her mom regarding her son's birth. The message still showed double ticks but hadn't turned blue. Determined, she decided to visit her mom's house and invite them to their grandson's naming ceremony. She took Brihant with her for support.

Standing outside the house, they knocked on the door. A woman answered but didn't invite them in. She asked, "Who are you?"

"I am Shadvika. Is my mom home?" she started to reply, but her brother arrived and asked, "Who is it, darling?"

Upon seeing his sister, he froze, anger flashing across his face. He shouted, "Why did you come back? Who told you to step into this house?"

In a calm tone, Shadvika replied, "Where are mom and Dad? I came here to see them."

"I don't need to answer your questions. Get out of my house," he shot back, slammed the door.

Anger surged within Brihant after witnessing his wife being disrespected. He began banging on the door again. Shadvika quickly intervened, calming him down as they stepped away. Just then, she heard a woman calling her name. Turning around, she noticed her neighbour, Meena Aunty, who was close to her mother, beckoning from a distance. Meena led them into her home, offering them a seat on the couch. "Six months ago, there was a severe fight between your sister-in-law and your mom. She slapped your mom and threw all her belongings out, then shut the door. After that, I haven't seen her. I don't know where she is, but I believe you could find her and take care of your parents, Shadvika," she said gently.

With a heavy heart, Shadvika left Meena's house. "Can you take me to another house of my parents? Let's check if they are there," Shadvika asked.

"Don't worry; we are not leaving for Italy without them. We will search everywhere," Brihant replied, hugging her for reassurance.

He took her to another house owned by her parents. Shadvika knocked on the door, and when it opened, she was confronted by the sight of her weakened, devastated mother. They stepped inside.

"Please come with us, Uncle and Aunty. I will take care of you," Brihant urged. Shadvika didn't speak; her eyes filled with tears at the sight of her parents alone.

"What happened, Mom? Please tell me everything," Shadvika insisted, emotion choking her voice.

"From the very first day after your brother's marriage, your sister-in-law and I didn't get along. I treated her like my own daughter, but she insulted me in front of everyone. She would shout at me for the smallest things. Your father retired, and we became dependent on your brother's salary. She ruled over me, believing it was her husband's money. Your brother supported her and abandoned us. Things became unbearable, and one day, she threw us out," her mother explained, her voice heavy with despair.

"Aunty and Uncle, pack your bags. You have a grandson! We came here for his baby naming ceremony, but I also plan to take you both with us to Italy. You don't have to struggle here; come on, let's leave," Brihant said earnestly.

With tears in his eyes, Shadvika's father replied, "Oh, my son! How we misunderstood you both. I trusted my wife's words and doubted my lovely daughter. I left her alone all these years, but you took care of her so well. Now you are here to take care of us. I didn't just get a son-in-law; God gifted me a son. May I call you as my son?" her father asked.

"What is this, Uncle? I will always be your son," Brihant responded warmly.

"Then call me Dad and your aunt Mom from now on, okay?" Mithan said with a smile.

With a shy smile, Brihant replied, “Okay, Dad.”

They packed their bags and left for the naming ceremony, giving their baby the name Hemanth. They enjoyed a week in India and then flew back to Italy with Mithan and Varnika.

In Italy, they lived a peaceful life. Shadvika, once a caged bird, was now free from her fears, misunderstandings, and pain. She soared higher alongside her family, ensuring that her parents never had to bow their heads in disappointment or shame again. Each day, she took care of her parents and showered them with joy and delights.

***

MONOLOGUE

This story may be fiction, but her reality is not. There are countless women around us, among us, still living behind invisible bars. Not all cages have locks or walls. Some are built from expectations, obligations, and judgments that quietly clip a woman's wings before she even learns to fly. These women shrink themselves day by day, sacrificing their dreams, their voice, their identity, for the sake of friendships, love, family, and society. And in doing so, they often forget who they are, or never truly discover what they're capable of.

This story is for them, for every woman who was told to be less, to stay silent, to accept blame that was never hers to carry.

When we think of a "caged woman," we often imagine someone who is not allowed to step out of her home, or someone denied education or freedom. But the truth is deeper, more painful, and far more common. A caged woman can be anyone, any woman who is misunderstood, repeatedly blamed, emotionally manipulated, judged for her choices, silenced when she speaks, or made to feel unworthy when she dreams.

This cage isn't always visible to the eye. It hides in the words that tell her to "adjust," in the tone that mocks her ambition, in the glances that shame her confidence. It exists in the fear of being labelled "too much", too bold, too emotional, too independent. Society often teaches women to shrink themselves so they can be accepted. To apologize for being strong, to doubt their worth simply because they don't fit someone else's idea of who they should be.

This story was written to say what many women have never had the chance to express: That a caged woman still dreams. She still hopes, still believes, still holds a fire within her, burning quietly behind her silence.

Some women fight for their dreams and break free, rising against all odds. But many fight inwardly, in isolation, and are forced to let go of their desires, not because they lacked strength, but because the world chose not to hear them.

Too often, women are judged for the way they dress, the way they talk, the way they carry themselves, or for daring to live life on their own terms. Society holds onto the belief that if a woman is given freedom, she will forget her responsibilities, become arrogant, or lose her family values. And yes, there may be a few who misuse freedom, but why must all women pay for the few? Not every woman is the same.

There are women who balance career and family with grace.
There are women who lead teams during the day and lullabies at night.
There are women who are firm in their boundaries and soft in their hearts.
There are women who are silent, not because they have nothing to say, but because no one ever truly listened.

So, if this story has touched something in you, I ask for just one thing:
Believe differently.
Listen more deeply.
Look beyond what you see.
Speak up for the women who have forgotten their own voices.
And when you see a woman being caged by guilt, judgment, or silence, **be the one who helps her find her way out.**

Let's uncage her. Not because she needs saving.
But because she deserves to soar.

ABOUT THE AUTHOR

Sudarshini is a passionate writer with a technical academic background. She began writing at the age of nine and is the founder and sole writer of *Glimmering Words*. She has authored multiple e-books and contributed as a co-author to several anthologies, most notably *Unsaid Words*, published by Writer's Pocket.

Her journey of inspiring minds through words began at the age of twelve. Her writing reflects her belief in the power of emotion, resilience, and silent strength, hoping to touch hearts and spark change, one word at a time.

To read more of her work, follow *Glimmering Words* on social media.